Dear Parent:
Your child's love of reading starts here!

Every child learns to read in a different way and at his or her own speed. Some go back and forth between reading levels and read favorite books again and again. Others read through each level in order. You can help your young reader improve and become more confident by encouraging his or her own interests and abilities. From books your child reads with you to the first books he or she reads alone, there are I Can Read Books for every stage of reading:

SHARED READING
Basic language, word repetition, and whimsical illustrations, ideal for sharing with your emergent reader

BEGINNING READING
Short sentences, familiar words, and simple concepts for children eager to read on their own

READING WITH HELP
Engaging stories, longer sentences, and language play for developing readers

READING ALONE
Complex plots, challenging vocabulary, and high-interest topics for the independent reader

ADVANCED READING
Short paragraphs, chapters, and exciting themes for the perfect bridge to chapter books

I Can Read Books have introduced children to the joy of reading since 1957. Featuring award-winning authors and illustrators and a fabulous cast of beloved characters, I Can Read Books set the standard for beginning readers.

A lifetime of discovery begins with the magical words "I Can Read!"

*Visit www.icanread.com for information
on enriching your child's reading experience.*

Adventures of
PADDINGTON

ADVENTURES OF PADDINGTON

Paddington Sets Sail
Text copyright © 2016 by Michael Bond
Illustrations copyright © 2016 by HarperCollins Publishers

Paddington and the Magic Trick
Text copyright © 2016 by Michael Bond
Illustrations copyright © 2016 by HarperCollins Publishers

Paddington Plays On
Text copyright © 2016 by Michael Bond
Illustrations copyright © 2016 by HarperCollins Publishers

Paddington's Day Off
Text copyright © 2017 by Michael Bond
Illustrations copyright © 2017 by HarperCollins Publishers

Stories adapted from the original Paddington stories written by Michael Bond.

I Can Read Book® is a trademark of HarperCollins Publishers.

ISBN: 978-0-06-274222-3
Manufactured in Dong Guan City, China
Lot#:
17 18 19 20 21 SCP 5 4 3 2
12/17

Adventures of
PADDINGTON

Michael Bond • illustrated by **R. W. Alley**

HARPER
An Imprint of HarperCollinsPublishers

Table of Contents

PADDINGTON
Sets Sail

Michael Bond
illustrated by R. W. Alley

One morning,

Mr. Brown had a surprise.

"We're taking a trip

to the beach!" he said.

Paddington, Jonathan, and Judy

cheered.

Mrs. Brown and Mrs. Bird
were excited, too.

Paddington had never been
to the beach.
He did not know what to bring,
so he packed everything.

Soon they were on their way.
Paddington poked his head
out the window.
He sniffed the salty sea air.

At the beach,
Paddington got a pail, shovel,
sunglasses, and a float.

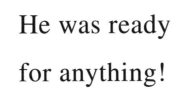

He was ready

for anything!

The tide was low,

so they went in the water.

Jonathan and Judy

splashed and swam.

Paddington floated in the waves.

At lunch,

Mr. Brown had a great idea.

He said, "Let's have

a sand castle contest!"

Paddington, Judy, and Jonathan
would each make a sand castle.
The biggest castle would win.

Paddington wanted to win.

First, he found a perfect spot.

He dug a moat.

He carried

pails and pails of sand.

He made walls and windows.

Paddington placed his hat
on top of the castle.
Finally, he was done.
Paddington's big sand castle
was perfect!

Paddington sat
inside his castle.
Sand castle work was hard
and he was tired.

Then he fell asleep.

Oh no!

The tide had come in!

It knocked down

Paddington's sand castle.

It carried Paddington's pail

out to sea—

with Paddington in it!

The Browns were worried.

It was getting late.

They found Paddington's hat
but could not find Paddington.
Where had he gone?

Then the Browns spotted
people gathered
near the pier.
They ran toward the crowd.

It was Paddington!

People believed

that Paddington had floated

all the way across the sea.

They took his picture.

"Did you float here in this pail?"
a girl asked.

"Yes. I used my shovel
as a paddle," said Paddington.

The sun was setting.

It was time to go home.

"Did you enjoy your trip,

Paddington?" asked Judy.

"Yes. Not many bears go to sea

in a bucket," he said.

The Browns were so happy
to have Paddington back.
"Today's trip was a bit shorter
than when you came
from Darkest Peru,"
said Mr. Brown.

Paddington did not hear.

He was fast asleep.

PADDINGTON
and the Magic Trick

Michael Bond
illustrated by R. W. Alley

It was Paddington's first birthday
since moving in with the Browns.
Everyone was getting ready
for the party.
Judy hung streamers.
Jonathan blew up balloons.

Paddington could hardly contain
his excitement.

Mrs. Bird baked a special cake
for the big day.
She filled it with marmalade
and covered it with icing.

Paddington wanted a taste.

Mrs. Bird let him lick the spoon.

It was the best birthday cake

he'd ever tasted!

Paddington went to look

at his presents.

He opened his new magic set.

He put on the hat and cape.

Paddington had a great idea!

He would perform at the party.

But first he had to learn

a few magic tricks.

Paddington waved the magic wand.

"Abracadabra!" he said.

He did not see his marmalade jar

drop into the secret drawer.

The trick worked!

Paddington practiced some more.
He couldn't wait to perform
for his guests.

Soon the guests arrived.

Paddington's good friend,

Mr. Gruber, led the way.

Everyone sang "Happy Birthday."
Then Paddington blew out
the candles on his cake.

49

It was time for the magic show.

Paddington set up

his magic box.

Jonathan and Judy
dimmed the lights.
Everyone was excited
to see Paddington perform.

Paddington put an egg

on the magic box.

He covered it with a scarf.

He said the magic word.

He waved his wand.

The egg had disappeared!

Paddington took a bow.

He tucked his paw

into the secret drawer

to get the egg.

Ta-da! It was . . . a jar.

Paddington was surprised.

How had a jar

ended up where the egg

was supposed to be?

Paddington's guests smiled

and waited for the next trick.

Next Paddington would make

flowers disappear.

But he could not remember

all the steps.

Paddington opened a large door
in the back of the box.

He crawled inside to check
the steps in his magic book.

His guests waited and waited.

Was this the trick?

Finally, Mr. Gruber

knocked on the box.

"Are you okay in there, Mr. Brown?"

Paddington was stuck!

Mr. Brown helped Paddington
out of the box.

"Maybe you could do
another kind of magic trick,"
Mrs. Brown suggested.

Paddington tried a card trick.

Mr. Gruber picked a card.

Paddington tore it
into little pieces.

"This part is tricky,"
said Paddington.
He covered the card
with his scarf.

Paddington waved the wand.
"Abracadabra!" he said.

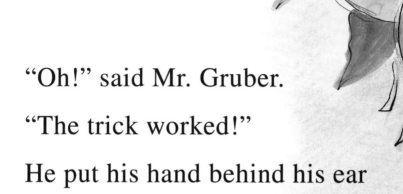

"Oh!" said Mr. Gruber.

"The trick worked!"

He put his hand behind his ear

and pulled out a coin.

Mr. Gruber handed him the coin.

Paddington knew just how

he would spend it.

He would buy their next

morning buns!

PADDINGTON
Plays On

Michael Bond
illustrated by R. W. Alley

Paddington and the Browns
took a trip to France.
The people in the village
were excited to meet a young bear.
The baker made buns
just for Paddington.
Other shopkeepers waved to him
when he walked through town.

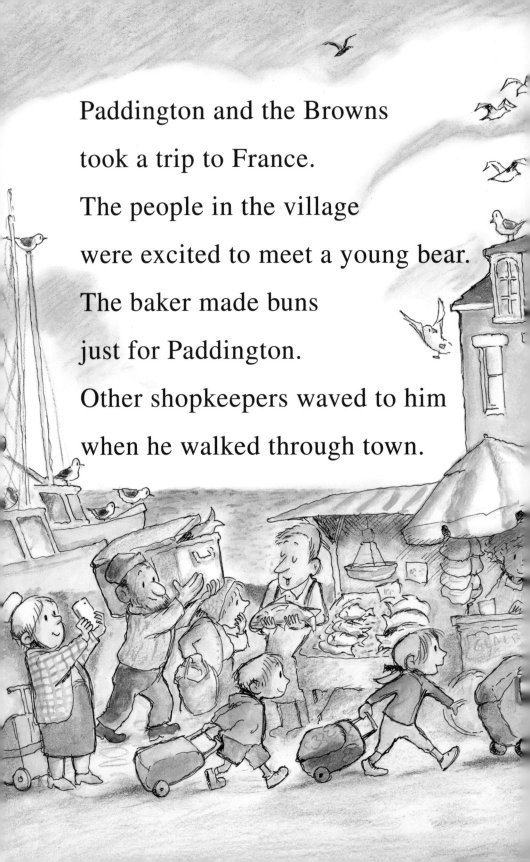

The next morning,

Paddington woke

to loud noises

in the street.

Paddington looked
out the window.
People were dressed
in fancy clothes.

The shops were decorated
with flags.
They were filled
with sweets and candles.

Paddington went to see the baker.

He told Paddington

all about a special festival

in the town.

That day, there would be a fair,

fireworks, and a parade!

"I am the leader of the band,

and this is my uniform,"

said the baker.

Paddington was very impressed.

Paddington and the Browns
went to the fair.
There was so much
to see and do!

Paddington tried

the slides and swings.

He rode the merry-go-round

over and over again.

Next Paddington visited
a fortune-teller.
She looked into her crystal ball.
"You will go on a journey.
It will end with a bang!"
she predicted.

When Paddington came
out of the tent
he saw the baker
looking worried.

The band's drummer
was too sick to drum.
They needed a replacement!

"The fortune-teller predicted
a big bang," Paddington said.
"This could be it."
Paddington would join the band!

Boom, boom, boom!
Paddington practiced
with the band
all afternoon.

The parade began that evening.
The baker led the band
down the street.
Paddington came last.
He carried a big drum.
He could not see over it.

But everyone saw Paddington!
The people were thrilled that he
was playing in the band.
He had saved the day!

Everyone clapped.

The Browns clapped the loudest.

Paddington beamed with pride.

The band turned

at the end of the street.

But Paddington kept marching.

He did not see the band turn.

He just kept playing his drum.

Paddington was tired.

His hat kept slipping

into his eyes.

He could not hear the band anymore.

The drum was getting heavy.

Paddington tripped and fell down.

He could not get up!

Thump, thump, thump.

Paddington kept drumming.

The Browns watched

the band pass by.

Where was Paddington?

They followed the sound of his drum.

They were so glad to find him!

Everyone was thrilled
to see Paddington.
They cheered for
their guest drummer.

Paddington and the Browns
settled in to watch
the evening show.
Fireworks!

Bang! The sky filled with colors.

Paddington beamed.

It was the perfect ending

to an eventful day.

PADDINGTON'S
Day Off

Michael Bond
illustrated by R. W. Alley

One day Paddington went
out for a walk.

He got out his basket on wheels
and put on his coat and hat.

He wanted to see his friend

Mr. Gruber, who owned a shop

in the Portobello Road market.

Mr. Gruber made them some cocoa.

Paddington had some buns to eat.

"It's such a beautiful day,"

Mr. Gruber said.

"Let's take the day off!"

Mr. Gruber closed up the shop.
Paddington hung a sign
on the door.

Paddington and Mr. Gruber

invited Jonathan and Judy

to come along, too.

They packed a lunch.

Paddington brought his suitcase,
a map, and his guidebook.

He also brought his opera glasses.

Mr. Gruber pointed out
lots of things as they passed
by stores and cafés.

Paddington stopped and said hello

to everyone they saw along the way.

Mr. Gruber led them
through a gate into a park.
Paddington was amazed.

VICTORIA PARK

IN THE
BANDSTAND
TODAY:

THE
GUARD'S
BAND

There was so much to see and do!

They stopped for lunch by the lake.
Paddington dipped his paws
into the water while he ate
his marmalade sandwich.

At the amusement area,
they played on the slide
and the swings.

Then Mr. Gruber said,

"What's that sound?"

They all stopped to listen.

They heard music playing.

They walked farther into the park

and found a little bandstand.

A band was playing!

Mr. Gruber found some empty chairs.

They all sat down.

Mr. Gruber read the program.

"They are playing

a famous Surprise Symphony!"

Paddington loved surprises.

He wondered what

the surprise would be.

Paddington decided to ask
the band about the surprise.
He walked around the bandstand.
There was a door marked "Private."
It opened easily.

Inside, Paddington looked around.

It was dark and dusty and gloomy.

The door closed behind him.

Paddington pushed on the door.

It wouldn't open!

Paddington found an old broom.

He pounded on the ceiling.

Mr. Gruber wondered
where Paddington had gone.
The music was playing.
It didn't sound right.

Bump, bump, bump!

The sound was coming
from under the stage.

Bump, BUMP, BUMP!
The conductor jumped.
The sound was coming
from under his feet.

The conductor reached down
and opened a door in the stage.

"Oh!" he exclaimed.

"It's a bear!"

The conductor helped Paddington
climb onto the stage.
"Would you like to finish
the Surprise Symphony?" he asked.
He handed Paddington his baton.

Paddington waved the baton
in the air and then took his bow.
Everyone clapped and cheered.
It was a surprising end
to a most enjoyable day off!